BEAR ON A BIKE

Written by Stella Blackstone
Illustrated by Debbie Harter

TED SMART

Bear on a bike,
As happy as can be,
Where are you going, bear?
Please wait for me!

I'm going to the market,
Where fruit and flowers are sold,
Where people buy fresh oranges
And pots of marigold.

Bear on a raft,
As happy as can be,
Where are you going, bear?
Please wait for me!

I'm going to the forest,
Where fearsome creatures prowl,
Where racoons play and bobcats snarl
And hungry foxes howl.

Bear in a steam train,
As happy as can be,
Where are you going, bear?
Please wait for me!

I'm going to the seaside,
Where children love to play,
Where young friends dig and race
And swim, while fishes dart away.

Bear on a boat,
As happy as can be,
Where are you going, bear?
Please wait for me!

I'm going to an island,
Where magic star fruits grow,
Where herons fish in secret groves
And sparkling rivers flow.

Bear in a carriage,
As happy as can be,
Where are you going, bear?
Please wait for me!

I'm going to a castle,
Where night is turned to day,
Where princes and princesses dance
And merry music plays.

Bear on a rocket,
Flying through the night,
Wherever you are going, bear,
Goodbye and goodnight!

Barefoot Books Ltd
PO Box 95
Kingswood
Bristol
BS30 5BH

This edition produced for The Book People Ltd,
Hall Wood Avenue, Haydock, St Helens WA11 9UL
First published in the United Kingdom in 1998 by Barefoot Books Ltd.

Graphic design by Jennie Hoare, Bradford on Avon
Colour reproduction by Unifoto, Cape Town
Printed and bound in Singapore by Tien Wah Press (Pte) Ltd

British Library Cataloguing-in-Publication Data:
a catalogue record for this book is available from the British Library

Hardcover ISBN 1 901223 78 7
Paperback ISBN 1 901223 54 X

1 3 5 7 9 8 6 4 2